Milli, Jack, and the Dancing Cat

Stephen Michael King

Philomel Books ~ New York

For Enja, Tanith & Luka, Joey & Danielle, Peter & Anke

A big thank-you to Michael Green

Text and illustrations copyright © 2003 by Stephen Michael King.
All rights reserved. This book, or parts thereof, may not be reproduced
in any form without permission in writing from the publishers.
First American Edition published in 2004 by Philomel Books,
a division of Penguin Young Readers Group, 345 Hudson Street,
New York, NY 10014. Philomel Books, Reg. U.S. Pat. & Tm. Off.
Published in Australia by Allen & Unwin. The scanning, uploading
and distribution of this book via the Internet or via any other means
without the permission of the publishers is illegal and punishable by law.
Please purchase only authorized electronic editions, and do not participate in
or encourage electronic piracy of copyrighted materials. Your support
of the author's rights is appreciated.
Published simultaneously in Canada.
Manufactured in China by South China Printing Co. Ltd.
The text is set in Throhand Ink.
Stephen Michael King used ink and watercolors for the illustrations in this book.
Library of Congress Cataloging-in-Publication Data   King, Stephen Michael.
Milli, Jack, and the Dancing Cat / Stephen Michael King.   p.   cm.
Summary: Two wandering minstrels, Jack and the Dancing Cat, help Milli
the shoemaker gain the self-confidence she needs to express her many creative talents.
[1. Creative ability—Fiction. 2. Self-confidence—Fiction. 3. Minstrels—Fiction.
4. Dance—Fiction. 5. Cats—Fiction.] I. Title.
PZ7.K58915Mi 2004   [E]—dc22   2003012345
ISBN 0-399-24240-6
10 9 8 7 6 5 4 3 2 1
First American Edition

Milli could take a thing
that was a nothing . . .

and make it . . .

a something!

She found things other people threw away . . .

forgotten things,

rusty things.

She cut them,

bent them,

pulled them apart,

and joined them
together in amazing ways.

Milli loved to take a straight piece
of wire and give it a wiggle,
or a simple square of cloth
and set it dancing in the wind.

"I wish I could be as free as you,"
she would say as the cloth floated in the breeze.

But she was never brave enough
to show anyone what she could really do.

So, instead of doing
what she loved most,

Milli spent her days
making shoes.

Brown shoes,

black shoes,

and plain, ordinary
work boots.

Day after day, night after night,
Milli dreamed that things would be different.

But each new day was the same as the one before.

Then one morning, two vagabond minstrels
from faraway places trudged into town . . .

Jack and the Dancing Cat.

People rushed and bustled here and there, never stopping long enough to notice anything even a little different.

"Just another town," said Cat. Jack nodded his head.

But as Jack and Cat walked, they suddenly
heard something unexpected.
Someone humming and the sound
of feet shuffling a rough old dance on a dusty floor.

"It's coming from that shoe shop," said Cat.

So they waltzed right in.
"I'm Jack," said Jack.
"I'm Cat," said Cat.
"Oh! I'm . . . I'm Milli," said Milli
in surprise, trying quickly to hide
her shuffling feet. "It looks as though
you two need some new boots!"
Cat showed her
their empty purse.

Jack spun around, tipped his hat, and smiled. "We would be delighted to teach you some new dances in exchange," he said with a bow. Milli giggled shyly and agreed.

Jack and Cat taught Milli
all the dances they knew.

They did tap

and jazz

and ballet.

They did the two-step,
the three-step,

and the tricky twisting
backward-sliding four-step.

Sometimes they just wobbled,

fooled around and floated,

or pretended they had branches,
like a tree.

Dancing made Milli feel

brave and free.

Milli loved her new friends
and all the odd things about them.
She wanted to surprise them
with more than just plain, ordinary boots.

So, she made instruments
with sounds that had never
been heard before,

and curly-toed shoes
covered in stars,
and purple satin slippers
with bells.

There were clothes to match,
patterned and painted by hand,
and sewn with care.

And while Milli was making
things for Jack and Cat . . .

she also made things for herself.

A soft, swirling dress
especially for dancing,

a fantastic water fountain,

and a wiggly, wonderful seat
to sit outside her front door.

Jack and Cat still had faraway places to explore,
but they stayed a little longer to help Milli make some changes.
When it was time for them to leave, Jack asked,
"Do you feel brave enough to show everyone what you can do?"

Milli was afraid. But only a little. So she danced
a little dance and hummed a little tune,
and she remembered how it feels to be brave and free.
"Yes," she said. "I'm ready for everyone to see."

And they did.
Milli's creations were so spectacular that people
came from far and wide. Even the townspeople
slowed down for a look.

And nothing, after that,
was ever the same as before.

Jack and the Dancing Cat set off,
taking all the extraordinary things
Milli had made for them,
and they soon became
the greatest wandering minstrels in all the land.

And Milli?

She never again

made a

plain,

ordinary

anything . . .

except maybe a nice cup of tea
whenever Jack and Cat danced into town.